Gail Hamilton

English Kings in a Nutshell

An aid to the memory

Gail Hamilton

English Kings in a Nutshell
An aid to the memory

ISBN/EAN: 9783337391638

Printed in Europe, USA, Canada, Australia, Japan

Cover: Foto ©Andreas Hilbeck / pixelio.de

More available books at **www.hansebooks.com**

ENGLISH KINGS IN A NUT-SHELL ❧ AN AID TO THE MEMORY ❧ BY GAIL HAMILTON

NEW YORK · CINCINNATI · CHICAGO

AMERICAN BOOK COMPANY

1893

PREFACE.

FOR a brief but happy moment my path once led along-side that of a Fair Ladye, a very little lady, who was studying English history, and was ever setting her world astir by asking if Henry the Third was the son of Henry the Second, or who came next to Edward the Fourth.

For her convenience, and, to be quite frank, for my own, I wrote these rhymes. The little lady has grown so learned now that she no longer needs them, but walks among kings and queens with equal step as one who has come to her own. Therefore I give them over to the little folk universal with my heartiest good will.

The verses include all the English monarchs, their relation to their successors, the time and length of each reign, and

3

one or two prominent events or prominent names that marked its course. Whoever commits the verses to memory will therefore have a convenient little epitome of English history always at command.

To the illustrations, for which I can claim no credit, I may be allowed to call attention. They are not only refined and delicate in point of art, but they are conceived and arranged in the true historic spirit. They not only repeat and intensify, but enlarge, the story of the text, and thus add a distinct and special value to my booklet. It is to gratify myself that I make this public acknowledgment to the artist.

I beg to call especial attention to the fact that these verses were written and published in another form in February, 1885.

GAIL HAMILTON.

JANUARY, 1893.

PART ✤ ✤
ONE ✤

William the
Conqueror.
1066—1087.

Battle of Hastings.

With a Saxon King's word and a Norman Duke's sword
Came WILLIAM THE CONQUEROR, leading his
    horde,
In ten sixty-six, —

William Rufus.

1087–1100.

Death of WILLIAM II

Walter Bobbett

                —twice crowned, to make sure
To his son, WILLIAM RUFUS, his throne should
    inure,—
A soldier, a statesman, a ruffian, whom fate
In the New Forest slew by the hand of his mate;
Brought to England a child, crowned in ten eighty-seven,
(If Heaven save the mark!) arrow-sent into heaven!

Henry I.

1100 — 1135·

WRECK OF
THE WHITE SHIP.

QUEEN MATILDA

Next **HENRY**, his brother,— husband, father, and son
Of Matilda, three women whose names were but one;
Called Beauclerc for his lore, yet at logical feud,
When not in alliance, with Anselm the Good.
He witnessed young Oxford fare forth to renown,
With the century's close receiving his crown;
But having no son, of his William bereft
By the waves, to his daughter his kingdom he left,
In the year thirty-five, as he fondly believed:
But, with all his fine learning, the King was deceived,

Stephen.

1135 — 1154.

W.B.

For sister Adela's son, STEPHEN, refused
To account himself other than very ill used;
And as England elected him, daughter Matilda
Found nothing but title-deeds whereon to build a
Firm throne for her race, through nineteen troubled years,
When Stephen, the winning but weak, calmed her fears
By departing this life;—

Henry II.

1154 — 1189.

QUEEN ELEANOR.

—and her own boy was reckoned
The sole King of England, as HENRY THE SECOND,
Of legal repute, with little to fleck it
But the ill-advised murder of Thomas à Becket.
His youngest son bad, and his oldest departed,
In the year eighty-nine he sank down broken-hearted;

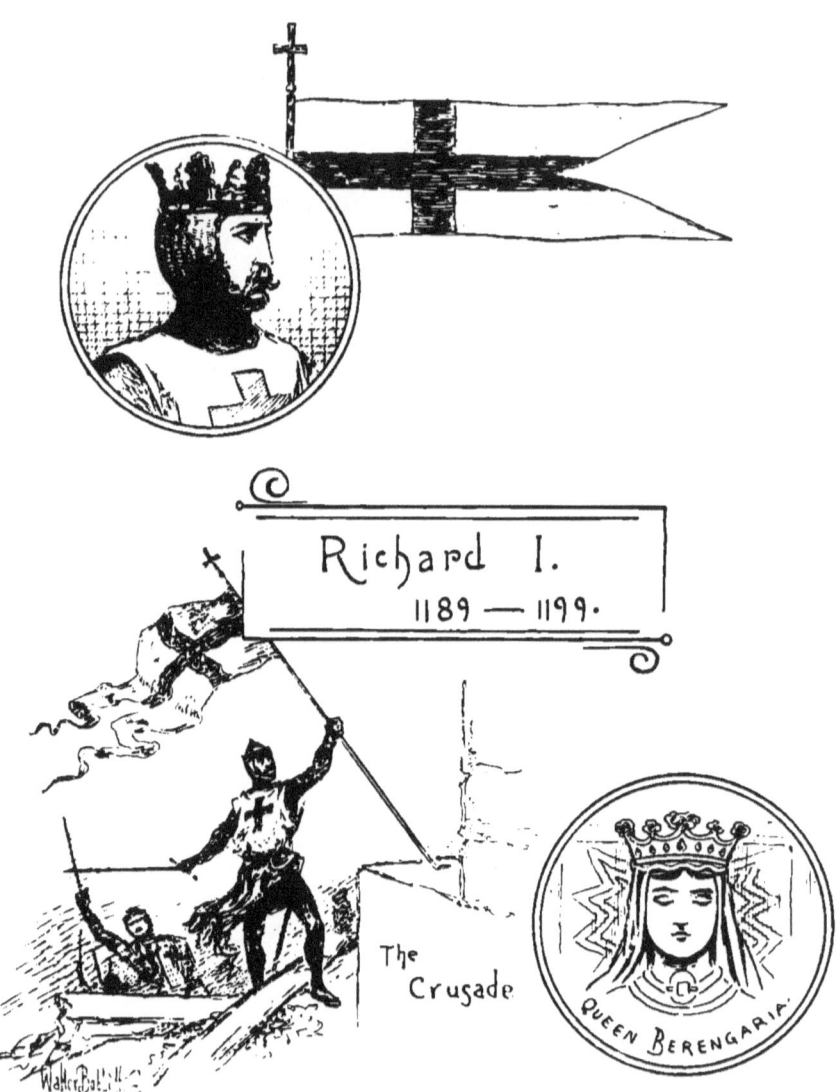

Richard I.

1189 — 1199.

The Crusade

QUEEN BERENGARIA

And RICHARD, his third son, rough, bluff absentee,
Came home twice to be crowned, then roamed off over sea;—
Crusader and captive, betrothed to young Alice,—
But bold Berengaria shared his sea-palace;
Not only the Heart but the head of a Lion,
He found, like his father, no home throne to die on;

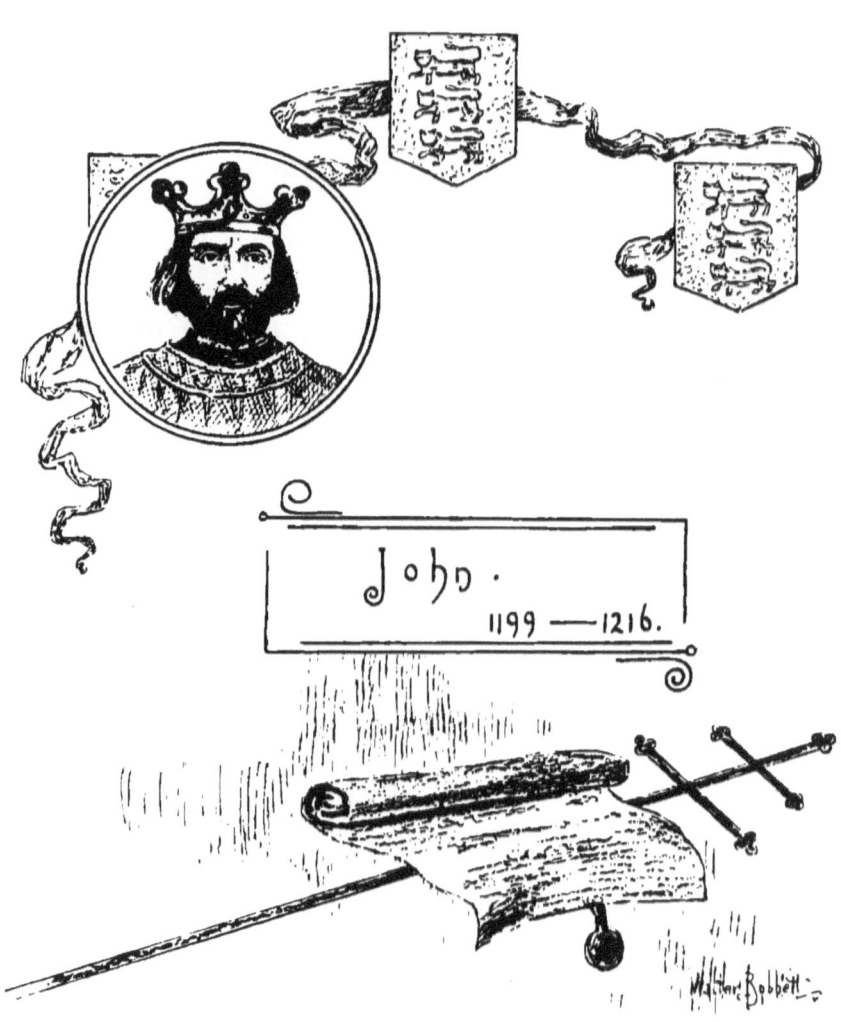

John.

1199 — 1216.

Whose death to his base brother JOHN power did bring,
Being thus, in ten years, third Plantagenet King.
Him his own barons forced all our freedom to cede,
When he signed Magna Charta at green Runnymede;

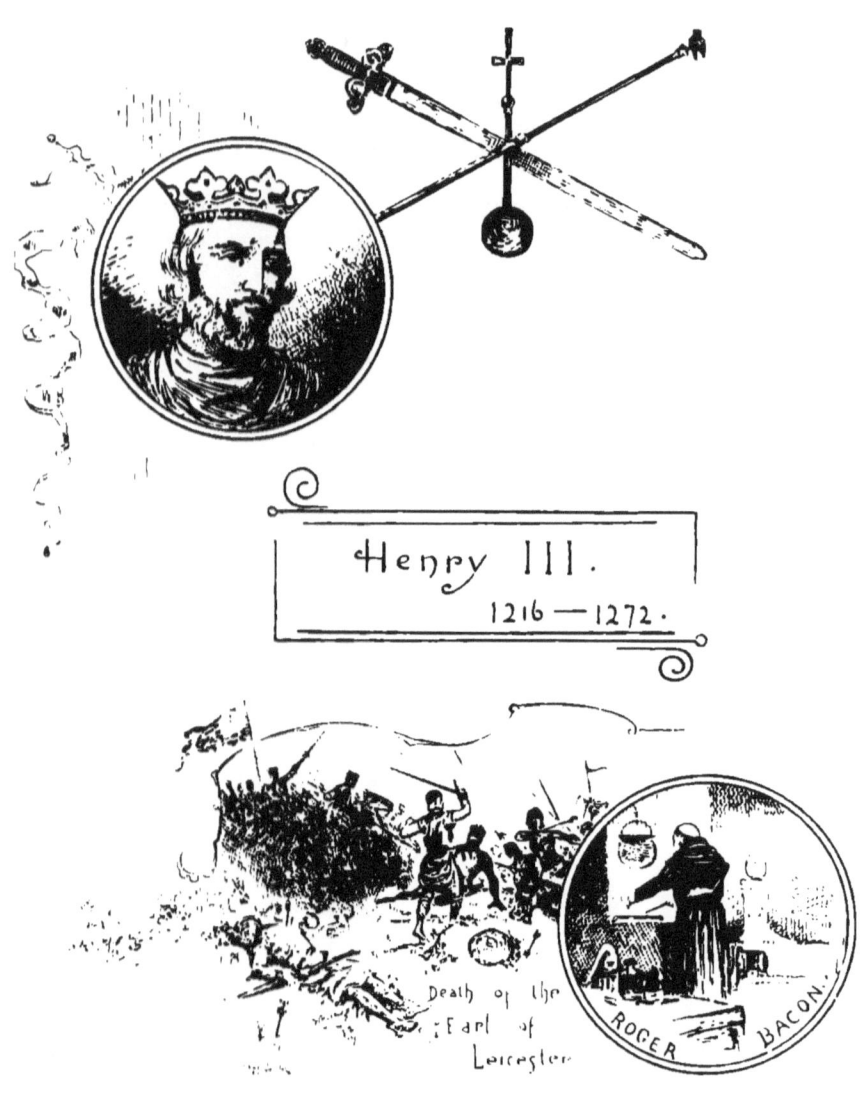

Henry III.

1216 — 1272.

Death of the
Earl of
Leicester

ROGER BACON.

But his fighting was stopped in twelve hundred sixteen,
And his small HENRY THIRD appeared on the scene.
Fierce quarrels with Leicester, his brother-in-law,
And prison and blood, his first forty years saw;

Edward I.
1272 — 1307.

Conquest of Wales.

— Walter Bobbett.

Then victorious peace until seventy-two,
When EDWARD, his son, came with all the ado
Of the warfares of Wallace and Balliol and Bruce,
With now and then triumph, and now and then truce,

Edward II.

1307 — 1327.

Battle of
Bannockburn.

Walter Robbett

Till the seventh year dawned of the centuries' teens,
And his son, EDWARD SECOND, on Isabel leans,—
A monarch most weak; but the curse of his life
Through his twenty years' reign was his Jezebel wife.

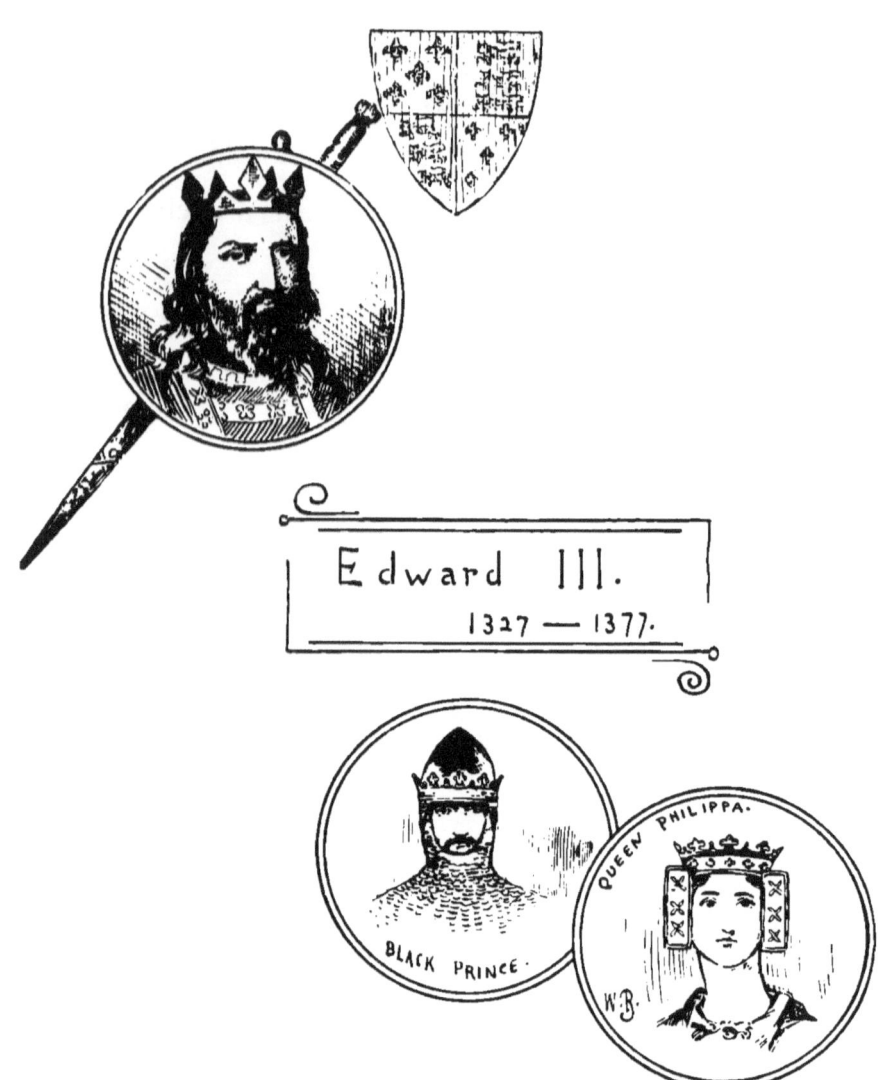

Edward III.
1327 — 1377.

BLACK PRINCE.

QUEEN PHILIPPA.

W.B.

Then his son, EDWARD THIRD, and Philippa the fair,
For fifty years fought at Crecy and Poitiers,
And o'er Balliol and Bruce; nor before then, nor since,
Braver warrior was seen than their son, the Black Prince,

Richard II.
1377 — 1399.

WAT TYLER

JOHN of GAUNT

Whose son, RICHARD SECOND, a minor, the rout
Of Wat Tyler put down, but himself was put out

Henry IV.

1399 — 1413.

CANTERBURY CATHEDRAL

By his own cousin Hal, in thirteen ninety-nine,—

John of Gaunt's son, King HENRY THE FOURTH
   of the line.

Fourteen years the old wars he fought in his turn,

And first gave the law that made heretics burn;

He built up the Church, not for God, but himself,

And the Commons made strong, not for right, but for pelf.

Yet he pensioned old Chaucer, be sure to remember,

And died like a saint in Jerusalem Chamber.

Henry V.
1413 — 1422.

Battle of Agincourt.

Walter Bobbett

His son, HENRY FIFTH, won at wild Agincourt,—

Brave soldier, pure statesman, what would you have more?

Henry VI.

1422 — 1461.

JOAN of ARC.

QUEEN MARGUERITE.

His son, HENRY SIXTH (in fourteen twenty-two
An eight-months-old babe), took his wife from Anjou,
Marguerite, but lost France through Orleans' brave maid;
Fought rebellion at home, was defied by Jack Cade;
Now prisoner, now king, through the wars of the Roses;
A pure, gentle scholar, in cloud his life closes;
Last legal Lancastrian.——

Walter Hobbis.

Edward IV.

1461 — 1483.

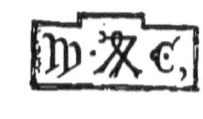

William Caxton.

   —Then to the throne
King EDWARD THE FOURTH bore the White Rose
  alone,—
Son of Richard of York, from third Edward descended;
But in twelve years he died, and his kingly line ended

Edward V.
1483 — 1483.

The Tower

By the murder of EDWARD THE FIFTH in the Tower,
With his poor little brother, in one midnight hour,

Richard III.
1483 — 1485.

Kaiser Robber?

Battle of Bosworth

That RICHARD THE THIRD, in fourteen eighty-three,
Their uncle, assassin, base monarch might be;
Though in two years, at Bosworth, his red sun went down,

Henry VII.
1485 — 1509.

Discovery of America.

And **HENRY THE SEVENTH** assumed England's
    crown.

A Welshman, a Tudor, an offshoot of Lancaster,

He flung off Bellona as far as man *can* cast her:

Piled up gold, wed the daughter of Edward the Fourth,

With his young Margaret bound King James of the North;

With his Henry the Eighth White and Red Roses blended:

And thus, to your joy, my long ditty is ended.

PART ✤ ✤
TWO ✤

Walter Bobbett.

Henry VIII.

1509 — 1547.

QUEEN
ANNE
BOLEYN

CARDINAL
WOLSEY.

Not so fast! I am ordered again to the fore;
And when kings must be rhymed, there are kings in galore.
In fifteen and nine **HENRY EIGHTH** brought the hope
Of peace, and wrenched England away from the Pope.
But fickle and savage and selfish, though able,
He slew his best friends, who ate salt at his table;
Killed two of six wives—if you think he was good,
With his loves and his murders, why, you have Mr.
    Froude!

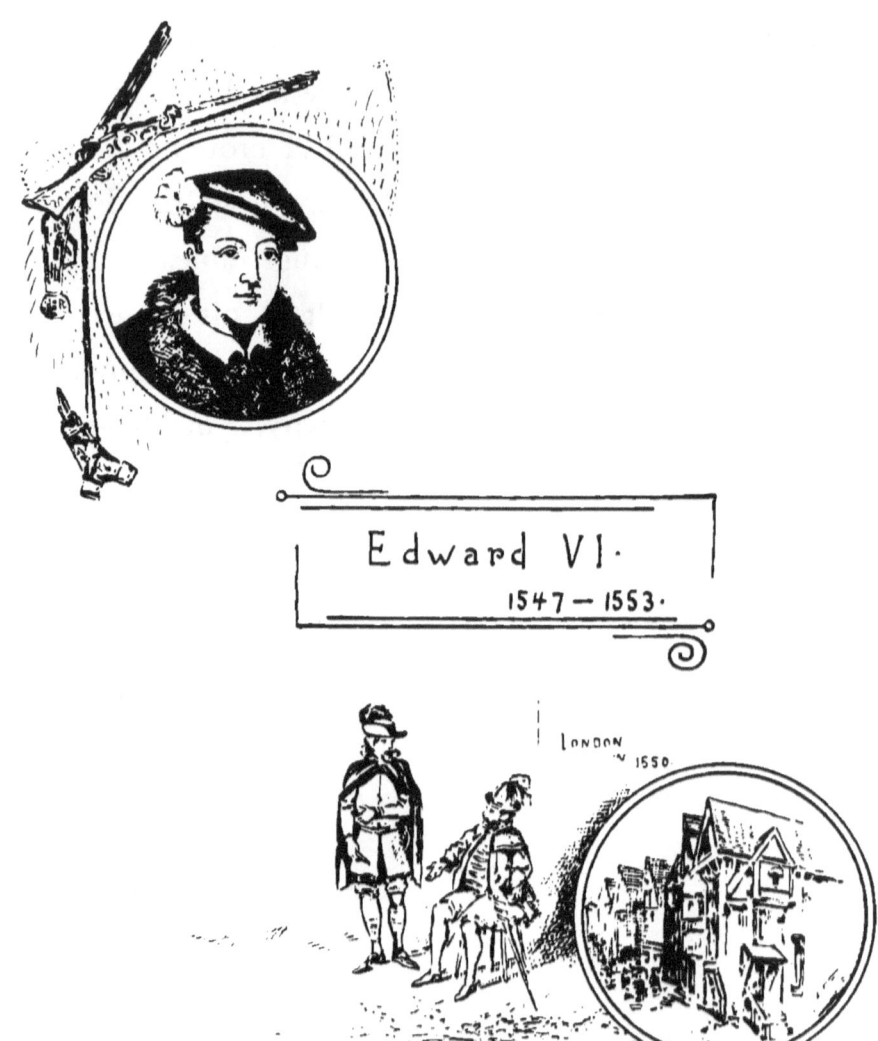

Edward VI·

1547 — 1553·

LONDON 1550

His son, **EDWARD SIXTH,** in fifteen forty-seven,
For six shining years rose, a star in our heaven;

Mary

1553 — 1558.

ROGER
ASCHAM

LADY JANE GREY.

Then his sisters,—poor **MARY**! ill-nurtured, ill-mated,
Learned, stupid, sincere, and right heartily hated,

The Armada.

Elizabeth
1558 — 1603.

MARY QUEEN OF SCOTS

Till the year fifty-eight; when uprose in her glory
ELIZABETH, Queen of all art, song, and story,
Proud maiden, great monarch. Ah! never a crown
On the brow of a man shone with brighter renown!
Strong-willed in the fire and the faults of her blood,
Old England yet knows her as Queen Bess the Good.

James I.

1603 — 1625.

Landing of the Pilgrims

The Gunpowder Plot.

JAMES FIRST, her far cousin, in sixteen and three,
Proved a Tudor diluted in Stuart to be,—
The rickety son of the Queen of the Scots.
He escaped from Guy Fawkes and his gunpowder plots;
Forced our Pilgrims and Puritans homeless to flee,
From his bigoted tyranny, over the sea:

Charles I.
1625 — 1649.

But when he expired, in sixteen twenty-five,

There were Puritans still left—at home and alive—

His son, **CHARLES THE FIRST**, to the scaffold to
   bring,

Who lied like a Stuart, but died like a king

Oliver Cromwell.
1653 — 1658.

MILTON.

In the year forty-nine, when forth with his sword
Came OLIVER CROMWELL, "the Scourge of the
    Lord."
Yet his country knows well that no king has bedecked her
With loftier bays than her sturdy Protector,—

Richard Cromwell.
1658 — 1660.

General Monk enters London.

General Monk.

Held her high for nine years; then the power he had won
Gave in death to the weak hand of **RICHARD**, his son,
Who cared not for honors, or army, or throne.

Walter Jobbitt

Charles II.
1660 — 1685.

Fire of London.

SIR ISAAC NEWTON.

So, in sixteen and sixty, came back to his own,

CHARLES SECOND, with welcome most loyal and
    glad, —

Kindly, careless, and witty, false, clever, and bad,

For twenty-five years, then died with urbanity:

James II.
1685 — 1688.

Flight of James II

And **JAMES SECOND,** his brother, devoid of humanity,
Dull, dogged, and cruel, sent Jeffreys to slaughter,
Himself soon sent right-about over the water.

William and Mary.
1689 — 1702.

Glencoe.

Remember the year of sixteen eighty-eight,
When his good daughter, MARY, and WILLIAM the Great
Of Orange, both Stuarts, born cousins, began
Fourteen years of freedom,—

Anne.
1702 — 1714.

Costume 1714

MARLBOROUGH

Walter Bubbott

—which simple QUEEN ANNE
Carried honestly on for a full dozen years;

George I.

1714 — 1727.

Costume 1715

Walter Bobbett

SIR ROBERT WALPOLE

Until brave **GEORGE THE FIRST**, the Elector, appears;
Not much of a king, but enough, it was granted,
To keep out the Stuarts,—the only thing wanted,—
Though the Stuart in Hanover blood was alone
The force that bore him to the proud island throne.

George II.

1727 — 1760.

French and Indian War

Waller Bobbett

WILLIAM PITT

Thus from twenty and seven to seventeen sixty,
His son, GEORGE THE SECOND, on the throne firmly
    fixed he,
Whose brave, stolid rule would have been far more sinister
If he had not been led by a wise wife and minister.

George III.
1760 — 1820.

The Surrender at Yorktown.

WASHINGTON

His grandson, **GEORGE THIRD**, the next sixty years
stood
In royal estate, stubborn, honest, and good.
We *should* be ungrateful to pass coldly by
The dear King who gave us our Fourth of July!

George IV.

1820 — 1830.

Canning.

PEEL.

Of his son, **GEORGE THE FOURTH,** the less said
    the better:
For his reign of ten years is Old England no debtor.

William IV

1830 — 1837.

Nor can **WILLIAM THE FOURTH** be thought over-
much given
To kingcraft, though King until thirty and seven.

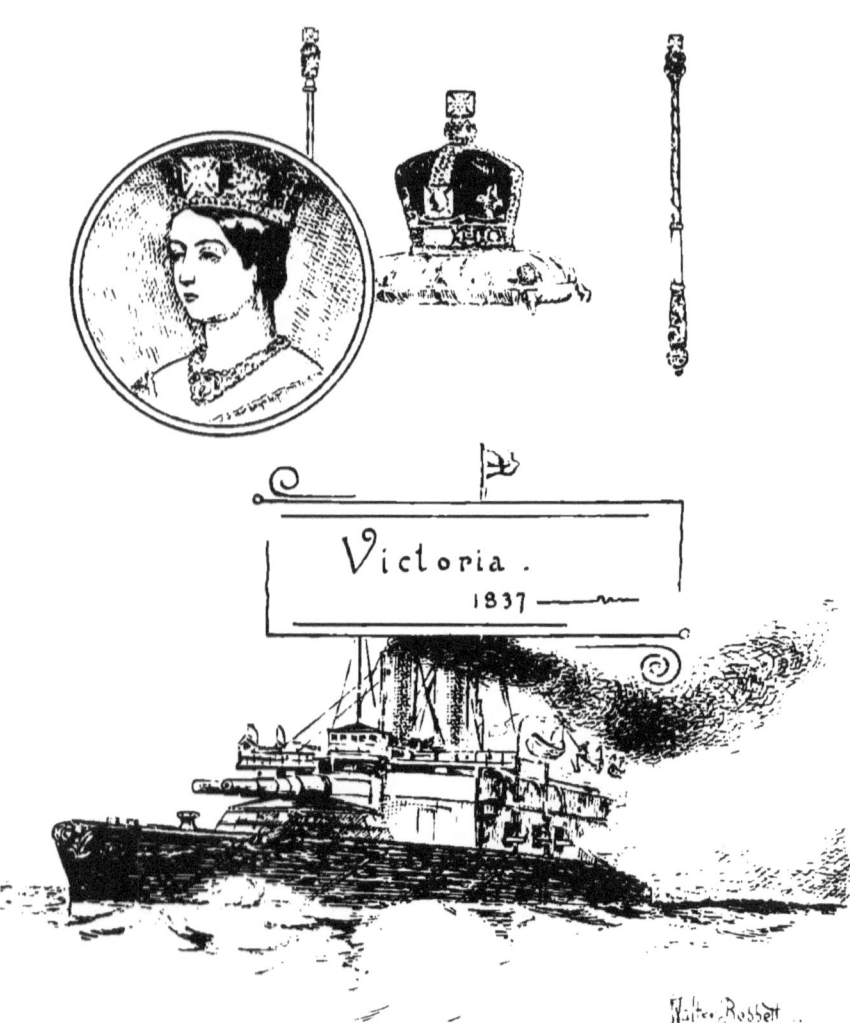

Victoria.

1837

Then welcome VICTORIA! heir of each grace
And each virtue that marked all the kings of her race;
Not alone in the East is she greatest and best,
We own the sweet sway of Victoria, West!
By her womanly worth, without contest or cost,
She has won back the empire her grandfather lost.
Her white hand was peace when our trouble was sore;
By that sign, she is queen of our hearts evermore.
The liegance of love sea nor sword shall dissever.
God's blessing be on her for ever and ever!

www.ingramcontent.com/pod-product-compliance
Lightning Source LLC
Chambersburg PA
CBHW032355020726
47499CB00008B/2761